TYRONE
THE
HORRIBLE

BY HANS WILHELM

SCHOLASTIC HARDCOVER

SCHOLASTIC INC. /New York

LIBRARY OF CONGRESS
Library of Congress Cataloging-in-Publication Data

Wilhelm, Hans, 1945-
Tyrone the Horrible / by Hans Wilhelm.
p. cm.

Summary: A little dinosaur named Boland tries several ways of
dealing with the biggest bully in the swamp forest, until
finally hitting on a successful tactic.
[1. Bullies—Fiction. 2. Dinosaurs—Fiction.] I. Title.
PZZ W64816Ty 1988
[E]—dc19
87-36461
CIP
AC

ISBN 0-590-41471-2

12 11 10 9 8 7 6 5 4 3 2 1   8 9/8 0 1 2 3/9

Printed in Italy   10
First Scholastic printing, September 1988

To Daniel

Boland was a little dinosaur.
He lived with his mother and father
in a great swamp forest.

There were a lot of dinosaur children
in Boland's neighborhood.

They played together every day,
and Boland was friendly with all of them —
all of them, except one....

His name was Tyrone — or Tyrone the Horrible, as he was usually called.

He was just a kid himself, but he was much bigger and stronger than most of the others.

He was a real bully if you ever saw one. In fact, he was the world's first big bully!

Tyrone especially liked to pick on Boland.
He punched and teased him and always
stole his snack or sandwich.

Boland tried to stay out of Tyrone's way,
but it seemed that no matter where he went,
Tyrone was waiting for him.

Night after night, Boland had a hard time getting to sleep.

He kept thinking of ways to avoid Tyrone.

It seemed hopeless.

Boland's playmates tried to help.

"You have to get Tyrone to be your friend,"
Terry said to Boland one day.

"That's easier said than done," said Boland.
"How do you make friends with someone who has been
hurting and teasing you all your life?"

"You have to give him a present and show
him you care," Terry said.

Boland thought for a while. What kind of present
could he give Tyrone? Then he remembered how
Tyrone was always taking his snacks and sandwiches.

"A present for Tyrone?" he said.
"Well, at least it's worth a try."

That afternoon, Boland went looking for Tyrone.
"Here," he said in his friendliest voice. "It's such a hot day,
I thought you might like a nice ice-cream cone."
Tyrone looked at Boland for a moment. Then
he smiled a nasty smile. "Ice cream for me?
How sweet!"

Tyrone grabbed the cone. Then he turned it upside down and squashed it on Boland's head.

"Ha ha ha!" Tyrone laughed and walked away.

Boland could hear Tyrone's laughter for a long time, echoing through the forest.

The next day, Boland told his friend Stella
what had happened.

"You are taking this too seriously," Stella said.
"Don't pay any attention to that big bully when he
tries to tease you. Just stay cool. That's the only thing
he'll understand."

"Staying cool when you are scared is not easy,"
Boland said. "But I will try."

And so the next time Boland met Tyrone, he stayed cool.

"Hi, Lizardhead!" roared Tyrone as Boland walked by. "How about MY sandwich?"

Boland did not pay any attention and didn't even try to run away. He kept on walking.

"I guess I'll have to help myself again," Tyrone said.
He stomped on Boland's tail until Boland let go
of the sandwich.

Boland tried not to show his tears. But it hurt a lot.

When Boland's friends found out what
Tyrone had done, they were furious.

"It's time to fight back!" Stego said. "Tyrone has
given you enough trouble. You must stand up to him
and show him you are a dinosaur, too. You can
win any fight against him. Tyrone just has a big
mouth, that's all."

Boland was angry, too. "You're right!" he said.
"Maybe I should fight him and stop this nonsense
once and for all."

"Well," Stego said, "let's do it right now!"

The four friends marched off to find Tyrone.

Boland stood up and faced Tyrone the Horrible.
"Listen, you brute," he said. "I have had enough
of your bullying. Come on and fight!"
Tyrone took one look at Boland, then grinned
and said, "Okay, if that's what you want."

It was a very short fight.
Little Boland had no chance against his big enemy.
"I'm sorry," Stego said. "That was not a very good
idea. You'd better give up. Some bullies you just
can't beat. You have to learn to live with them,
whether you like it or not."

But Boland did not like it.
"There just has to be a way to beat a bully,"
he thought.

He was still thinking as the moon came out
and the stars filled the sky. Suddenly he smiled
a big smile.

"That's it!" he said to himself.
Then he curled up and was soon fast asleep.

The next morning Boland took his sandwich and went off into the swamp forest as usual. It wasn't long before he ran into Tyrone.

"Another snack for me?" roared Tyrone. "I hope it's something good!" And with that he swiped the sandwich out of Boland's hand and swallowed it with one big gulp.

Boland walked on as fast as he could.

Suddenly he heard a terrible scream.

"AAaaaaaarghhhhhh!" It was Tyrone.
Huge flames were coming out of his mouth.
"HELP, I'm burning," he cried. "I'm dying!"
I'm poisoned! HELP, HEEEEEEELP!"

"Nonsense!" Boland said with a laugh. "It was only a sandwich. I didn't know you were so sensitive. I happen to like double-thick-red-hot-pepper-sandwiches. Too bad you don't." He turned around and went off, leaving the moaning and groaning Tyrone behind.

From then on, Tyrone stayed as far away from
Boland as he could.

Boland played happily with his friends in the
swamp forest all day, and he never had trouble falling
asleep at night.

When much, much later some
scientists found Tyrone the Horrible,
he looked a little different —
but he still had that nasty smile on his face.